ABC

for
JBY

Other books by Quentin Blake

PATRICK
JACK AND NANCY
ANGELO
SNUFF
MISTER MAGNOLIA
QUENTIN BLAKE'S NURSERY RHYME BOOK
THE STORY OF THE DANCING FROG
MRS ARMITAGE ON WHEELS

Illustrated by Quentin Blake
with text by Roald Dahl

THE ENORMOUS CROCODILE
REVOLTING RHYMES
DIRTY BEASTS
THE GIRAFFE AND THE PELLY AND ME

with text by Russell Hoban

HOW TOM BEAT CAPTAIN NAJORK
AND HIS HIRED SPORTSMEN
A NEAR THING FOR CAPTAIN NAJORK

Quentin Blake's
ABC

JONATHAN CAPE
THIRTY-TWO BEDFORD SQUARE LONDON

A B C D
E F G H
I J K L
M N O P
Q R S T
U V W X
Y Z

Aa

A is for Apples,
some green and some red

Bb

B is for Breakfast
we're having in bed

Cc

C is for Cockatoos
learning to scream

Dd

D is for Ducks
upside down in a stream

Ee

E is for Egg
in a nest in a bush

Ff

F is for Firework –
it goes BANG and WHOOSH

Gg

G is for Grandma –
she's really quite fat

Hh

H is for Hair
that goes under your hat

Ii

I is for Illness
(which *nobody* likes)

Jj

J is for Junk –
rusty beds and old bikes

Kk

K is for Kittens,
all scratching the chair

Ll

L is for Legs
that we wave in the air

Mm

M is for Mud
that we get on our knees

Nn

N is for Nose –
     and he's going to sneeze!

Oo

O is for Ostrich
who gives us a ride

Pp

P is for Parcel –
let's guess what's inside

Qq

Q is for Queen
with a cloak and a crown

Rr

R is for Roller skates –
watch us fall down!

Ss

S is for Sisters,
  some short and some tall

Tt

T is for Tent
where there's room for us all

Uu

U is Umbrella
to keep off the rain

Vv

V is for Vet,
   when your pet has a pain

Ww

W is for Watch –
we can hear the ticktocks

Xx

X is the ending
for jack-in-the-boX

Yy

Y is for Yak –
    he's our hairiest friend

Zz

Z is for Zippers
That's all
That's the end

Quentin Blake's ABC
First published 1989
Text and illustrations © 1989 by Quentin Blake
Jonathan Cape Ltd, 32 Bedford Square, London WC1B 3SG

A CIP catalogue record for this book
is available from the British Library

ISBN 0 224 02617 8
Printed in Italy by
Arti Grafiche Motta S.p.A.–Milan